The Tiara Club
at Pearl Palace

For Sarah, with love,
admiration, and huge thanks
VF

With special thanks to JD

www.tiaraclub.co.uk

ORCHARD BOOKS
338 Euston Road, London NW1 3BH
Orchard Books Australia
Level 17/207 Kent St, Sydney, NSW 2000

A Paperback Original
First published in 2007 by Orchard Books

Text © Vivian French 2007
Cover illustration © Sarah Gibb 2007
Inside illustrations © Orchard Books 2007

A CIP catalogue record for this book is available
from the British Library.

ISBN 978 1 84616 503 0

1 3 5 7 9 10 8 6 4 2

Printed in Great Britain

The paper and board used in this paperback are natural recyclable
products made from wood grown in sustainable forests.
The manufacturing processes conform to the environmental
regulations of the country of origin.

Orchard Books is a division of Hachette Children's Books,
an Hachette Livre UK company.

www.orchardbooks.co.uk

The Tiara Club

at Pearl Palace

Princess Sarah

and the Silver Swan

By Vivian French

ORCHARD BOOKS

The Royal Palace Academy
for the Preparation of Perfect Princesses

(Known to our students as "*The Princess Academy*")

OUR SCHOOL MOTTO:
*A Perfect Princess always thinks of others
before herself, and is kind, caring and truthful.*

Pearl Palace offers a complete education for
Tiara Club princesses with emphasis on the arts
and outdoor activities. The curriculum includes:

*A special Princess
Sports Day*

*A trip to the Magical
Mountains*

*Preparation for the
Silver Swan Award
(stories and poems)*

*A visit to the King
Rudolfo's Exhibition of
Musical Instruments*

Our headteacher, King Everest, is present at all times,
and students are well looked after by the head fairy
godmother, Fairy G, and her assistant, Fairy Angora.

Our resident staff and visiting experts include:

*QUEEN MOLLY
(Sports and games)*

*LADY MALVEENA
(Secretary to King Everest)*

*LORD HENRY
(Natural History)*

*QUEEN MOTHER MATILDA
(Etiquette, Posture and
Flower Arranging)*

We award tiara points to encourage our Tiara Club princesses towards the next level. All princesses who win enough points at Pearl Palace will be presented with their Pearl Sashes and attend a celebration ball.

Pearl Sash Tiara Club princesses are invited to go on to Emerald Castle, our very special residence for Perfect Princesses, where they may continue their education at a higher level.

PLEASE NOTE:
Pets are not allowed at Pearl Palace.
Princesses are expected to arrive at
the Academy with a *minimum* of:

TWENTY BALLGOWNS
*(with all necessary hoops,
petticoats, etc)*

TWELVE DAY DRESSES

*SEVEN GOWNS
suitable for garden parties,
and other special
day occasions*

TWELVE TIARAS

*DANCING SHOES
five pairs*

*VELVET SLIPPERS
three pairs*

*RIDING BOOTS
two pairs*

*Cloaks, muffs, stoles, gloves
and other essential
accessories as required*

Hello! I'm Princess Sarah!
Do you ever get into a panic about
things at the last minute? I do! When
I realised it was almost the end of term,
I went hot and cold. Luckily my friends
from Lily Room are very good at calming
me down. I don't know what I'd do
without Hannah, Isabella, Lucy,
Grace and Ellie...and you.

Chapter One

Does it get extra busy in your school when it's nearly the end of term? It did at Pearl Palace. All of a sudden the teachers were pinning our work on the walls, and complaining if we hadn't finished our projects. In Lily Room we'd been working on Magical Animals, and we'd drawn loads of pictures of dragons and unicorns. Hannah and Lucy had written stories, and Isabella, Grace and Ellie had done legends. I said I'd make up a poem – but I STILL hadn't thought of any words!

The harder I tried, the more I couldn't think of anything. Diamonde and Gruella, the horrible twins, kept asking me how I was getting on, and sniggering when I said I hadn't finished yet. They'd written a really REALLY long poem about two princesses who were so beautiful that princes came from miles around to ask them to marry them.

"We're going to recite our lovely poem after we've won the Silver Swan Award," Diamonde said smugly.

I hadn't heard of the Silver Swan Award, so I asked Lucy what it was. She reads the notice board every day, which is just as well because I nearly always forget to look.

"It's a special prize for the princess – or group of princesses – who have done the most to make other people happy during their time at Pearl Palace," she said.

"Oh," I said. I couldn't quite believe the twins had ever made anyone happy, but I didn't think it would be very princessy to say so.

"You know we only get given our Pearl Sashes if the magical Silver Swan flies down to the Pearl Palace lake?" Lucy asked, and I nodded. "Well, after that happens – IF it happens – King Everest announces the winners of the award, and they lead the procession to the Pearl Palace ballroom."

"Oh," I said for the second time. I was beginning to feel worried. Our school fairy godmother,

Fairy G, had already told us all about the magical swan, and how she wouldn't come if we didn't deserve to win our sashes. I couldn't help wondering – if I didn't get my poem written, would that mean I didn't deserve a sash? And would that stop the swan coming for everybody else?

I got up early every morning for a week, but however often I muttered "De dum de dum, de dum de dum," no words came. Ellie had a couple of ideas, but of course I couldn't use them.

"You don't have to be a Perfect Princess ALL the time," Isabella said. "No one would know Ellie thought of the idea – it'd still be your words."

"I'm sure the magic swan will know," I said gloomily. "Both Fairy G AND Fairy Angora keep saying it knows everything..."

I stopped. I'd FINALLY had an idea. I'd write my poem about the magic Silver Swan!

Even though I'd had an idea, I still didn't get my poem written. Our headteacher, King Everest, said he wanted us to welcome the Silver Swan with a special dance, and he kept arranging rehearsals in our free time. Whenever I thought I had ten minutes to find a rhyme for "swan" or "beautiful" I'd discover I was meant to be working on a project with everyone else.

And then something really DREADFUL happened!

Chapter Two

I was sitting with my friends after supper, when Diamonde and Gruella suddenly appeared right beside us.

"Have you written your poem yet?" Diamonde asked me.

"Erm...sort of," I said.

Diamonde raised her eyebrows.

"Dear me! Gruella and I have

just written another hundred lines
of OUR poem."

"Good for you." I tried to give
her a Perfect Princess smile (a
Perfect Princess always rejoices in
the success of others) but it didn't
work very well.

Ellie frowned. "Let me tell you,
Diamonde," she said, "Sarah's
fantastic at writing poems. She's
writing this totally brilliant poem
about the Silver Swan—"

And that's when we noticed our
headteacher was standing right
behind us.

"A poem about the Silver Swan,
Sarah?" he said. "That sounds an

excellent idea." He stroked his beard thoughtfully. "When the swan flies down you can read out your poem, and we'll have the welcome dance afterwards. Perfect! Come and see me on Friday after lessons, and show me what you've written. Good girl!"

He was about to stride away when Diamonde burst out, "But Your Majesty! Sarah hasn't even finished her poem! Gruella and I have written a MUCH better one, and it's all about two beautiful princesses—"

King Everest stopped her with a wave of his arm. "But is it about the Silver Swan?"

"Erm..." Diamonde hesitated. "Not exactly..."

"Then it's not very suitable, is it?" And this time King Everest did stride off, and Diamonde was left looking absolutely FURIOUS.

"That's SO not fair!" she hissed at me. "Just you wait!" And she grabbed Gruella, and rushed away.

"Ooops," Ellie said as the door swung shut behind them. "I didn't know King Everest was listening. I'm really sorry, Sarah."

"What for?" I asked. "Gruella and Diamonde are always fussing about something or other..."

My voice died away as I realised what Ellie was talking about, and the awful truth hit me. Not only was I going to have to write my poem by Friday, but King Everest was expecting me to read it out loud in front of EVERYONE on Saturday!

"Oh help," I said feebly, and I found myself almost hoping the Silver Swan would give Pearl Palace a miss this time.

The next day absolutely whizzed by, and I didn't get any further with my poem. And then it was Thursday, and I was SERIOUSLY beginning to panic. Normally we have a free period first thing, but King Everest announced we were going to have one last dance rehearsal – so instead of having a peaceful forty minutes in the library, I found myself outside by the lake. Fairy Angora was taking the rehearsal, and King Everest had sent along the Pearl Palace musicians. The music was so fabulous it made my feet twitch – but my mind was so busy trying to write a poem I made mistake after mistake. If I hadn't had Grace

hissing "Twirl NOW!" in my ear
I think Fairy Angora would have
given me about a million minus
tiara points.

As the bell went for break she called me out of line, and I was sure she was going to tell me off – but she looked anxious rather than cross.

"Are you all right, Sarah?" she asked as my friends filed past me on their way back into school. "You're usually so good at dancing."

I opened my mouth to explain, but instead I did something I've NEVER done before – I burst into tears!

"Oh no!" I wailed. "I'm so very sorry – I didn't mean to cry! It's just that I can't write my poem, and I've got to read it to King Everest tomorrow!"

Fairy Angora handed me a hankie, and waited while I blew my nose. "It sounds as if you could do with a little thinking time," she said. "Why don't you have a quiet walk round the lake, and see if that gives you any ideas."

"That would be really lovely," I sniffed. "Thank you so much."

Fairy Angora gave me a cheery wave and followed Diamonde and Gruella, who were at the end of the line. I could see Diamonde craning round to stare at me, but I turned and walked away.

Chapter Three

I felt better at once. The water was the most beautiful blue, and two butterflies were playing hide and seek in and out of the rushes. They seemed so happy I began to smile...and suddenly words came rushing into my head. I fished in my bag for a pencil and paper, sat myself down on the grass, and began to write.

Silver Swan, we welcome you
Flying down to water blue.
Butterflies and frogs and fishes
Watch as you bring us your wishes.
Pearl princesses raise a cheer

As you swoop and settle here –
Please accept our grateful thanks
As we stand upon the banks...
Flying down to water blue –
Silver Swan, we welcome you!

As I wrote the final exclamation mark I felt SO much better. I put my paper in my pocket and hurried away to the art room for my next lesson. I was half way up the stairs when I met Diamonde coming down.

"Oh, it's poor little crybaby Sarah," she sneered. "Did poor diddums get all upset because she can't write an ickle pitty swan poem, then?"

"Actually," I said as politely as I could, "I've written it. I'm just going to copy it out neatly." And I marched on past her.

Fairy G was taking the art lesson, and all the tables were covered in pictures.

"Ah! Sarah!" she boomed. "I'm getting the end-of-term display ready. I've sent Diamonde to fetch some pins, and when she gets back you can all help me put it up on the walls."

"Brilliant," I said. "But please may I copy out my poem first? I've got to read it to King Everest tomorrow."

"No problem." Fairy G beamed at me. "I'll find you some special paper. Would you like to use a quill pen and real ink?"

"Oh, yes PLEASE!" I said, and I carried the bottle of ink and the box of feather quills carefully to my table while Fairy G hunted in a cupboard. When she found the paper it was SO pretty: pale pink, with tiny flowers scattered over it.

As soon as she saw it, Gruella put up her hand. "Please, Fairy G," she asked, "can Diamonde and I have some too? We've written a poem about princesses, and Diamonde says it's the best poem ever."

Fairy G's eyebrows whizzed up her forehead, but all she said was, "Fancy that. Sarah dear, would you mind sharing with Gruella?"

"Of course not," I said. Gruella smiled a thank you, and the two of us began copying our poems.

We'd almost finished when Diamonde came back, and she rushed over to see what Gruella and I were doing.

"That's messy, Gruella," she said. "Let ME do the poem. My handwriting's LOADS better than yours." And she pushed Gruella out of the way.

Don't you just HATE it when someone behaves like that? I do, and for once Gruella SO didn't deserve it.

I looked at her. "Aren't you going to stand up for yourself?" I asked.

For a moment I thought she was

going to, but she didn't. She gave
me a funny half smile and moved
away. Diamonde sat down in her
place. There wasn't anything else
I could do, so I concentrated on
finishing my poem.

"That looks very nice, Sarah."
Fairy G was looking over my
shoulder. "You'd better leave it to
dry on the shelf. That ink takes
ages – and you don't want to get
smudges on it."

I did as I was told, and then
I went to help sort out the

pictures. Fairy G showed us where to pin them on the wall, and we had SUCH fun chatting and laughing that when the bell went I completely forgot about my poem. It wasn't until much later in the day that I realised I'd left it behind, but I wasn't worried. It would be safe in the art room.

"I'll fetch it before I go to bed," I told myself...but then Rose Room challenged us to a game of table tennis, and I forgot again. It was only when I was tucked up in Lily Room that night that I remembered.

"Bother," I said loudly, and Lucy sat up in bed with a start.

"What's the matter?" she asked.

"I've forgotten to fetch my poem from the art room," I said.

Grace sat up as well. "It'll be fine," she said. "But I meant to tell you – I found your rough copy when we were clearing up. I put it somewhere...oh, I know! It's in my dress pocket!" She hopped out of bed and rummaged about in the clothes on her chair. "Here it is!" And she handed me the first draft I'd written by the lake. "I really like it, by the way."

"Come on! Read it out, Sarah,"

Ellie demanded.

"Oh, PLEASE do!" Isabella begged, and Hannah added, "Pretty please!"

I could feel myself going red, but I did my best, and at the end all my friends clapped.

"That's fabulous." Ellie smiled.

"*Silver Swan, we welcome you...*"

Hannah immediately chimed in. "*Flying down to water blue!*"

And before I knew what was happening my friends had recited my whole poem back to me!

"See?" Lucy said. "That shows it's good. We learnt it at once."

There was a loud banging on the door, and Fairy G boomed, "NO TALKING!"

"Sorry, Fairy G!" we called back, and we settled down to go to sleep.

Chapter Four

As soon as breakfast was over the next morning I dashed up to the art room and collected my poem from where I had left it lying on the shelf. Fairy G had rolled it up neatly and tied it with a pink ribbon, and it looked SO smart! I tucked it into my school bag, and hurried off to my first lesson – *Banquets, and How to Cope with Fussy Eaters.* The morning whizzed by, and although I did mean to read my poem again to check for mistakes I didn't have time. Lunch was hectic too, as Fairy G and Fairy Angora came in with loads of lost property, and in the afternoon we had dance classes in the Pearl Palace ballroom.

Before I knew it, lessons were over for the day, and I was standing outside King Everest's study door to read my poem to him. I suddenly realised my knees were wobbly. King Everest called,

"Come in," and I turned the handle and went inside.

"Aha! Princess Sarah!" Our headteacher smiled at me. "Let's hear what you have to say about the Silver Swan."

I took a deep breath, unrolled my scroll with a flourish...

And stared.

The paper was completely blank. I tried desperately to remember what I'd written, but somehow it all got jumbled up in my head – and when King Everest began to tap with his fingers on his desk it made it ten million times worse.

"Silver Swan, on water blue..." I stammered. "I mean, 'Silver Swan, we thank you...'"

King Everest stood up, and he was frowning. "Princess Sarah, have you written a poem at all?"

"Oh YES, Your Majesty," I said. "But...but I...I've brought the wrong piece of paper...I'm so very very sorry..."

King Everest stared down at me. "I'm disappointed, Sarah. VERY disappointed. I'd always thought of you as a clever girl, but this is ridiculous. And extremely careless as well. You do NOT deserve to welcome the Silver Swan. I shall ask the twins to read their poem instead. Please take ten minus tiara points!" And then he held open the door, so all I could do was make my way out, my face burning.

As I trailed along the corridor I couldn't help thinking the lovely Silver Swan was absolutely BOUND to miss her visit to Pearl Palace this year...and it would be all my fault.

My friends didn't agree at all. When I told them what had happened, and showed them the piece of pink paper, they were FURIOUS.

"You have to tell Fairy G," Hannah said. "Diamonde MUST have swapped it!'

"'Perfect Princesses never tell tales,'" I sighed. "And maybe it wasn't Diamonde after all.

Maybe I picked up the wrong piece of paper?"

"Of course it was Diamonde." Lucy sound fierce.

Isabella looked at Grace. "Couldn't we tell King Everest it wasn't Sarah's fault?"

Grace shrugged. "You know what grown-ups are like. He'd only say Sarah should have checked her poem before she came to his study, or something like that."

"Oh dear," Ellie said sadly, "and it's such a lovely poem."

And then the bell went for tea, and we had to go.

I didn't sleep at all well that night. I kept wondering what would happen if the Silver Swan didn't come. If we didn't get our Pearl Sashes, would that mean we couldn't go to Emerald Turrets next term? I tossed and turned, and when it was time to get up I felt dreadful. I couldn't eat any breakfast, or lunch, and by the time King Everest announced that it was time to go out into the Pearl Palace gardens to wait for the arrival of the Silver Swan, I felt horribly sick.

Diamonde flounced up to me as I took my place with my friends.

"I'M going to read a PROPER poem," she jeered.

"Isn't Gruella going to read it with you?" I asked.

Diamonde stuck her nose in the air. "I read MUCH better than she does," she said.

"That doesn't seem very fair." I folded my arms. "After all, you both wrote it, didn't you?"

Diamonde didn't answer. She marched away, and I suddenly found Gruella standing right beside me.

"Sarah," she whispered, "what happened when you went to read your poem to King Everest?"

I stared at her. "Why?"

"PLEASE tell me!" she begged.

"I unrolled my poem, and it was a blank piece of paper," I told her.

"OH!" Gruella gave a funny little squeak. "That's SO mean of her! She's AWFUL!"

The next thing I knew she was running across the grass towards Fairy G, but before I could see what happened next there was a loud shout from someone in the crowd.

"Look! LOOK! I can see the Silver Swan!"

Chapter Five

We gazed into the sky. At first I couldn't see anything, but Grace nudged me and pointed, and there she was – a tiny silver speck in the distance. Gradually she flew nearer and nearer, and I think every single one of us was holding our breath. Would she fly down? Or was she going to fly past?

She didn't do either. She began
to circle round and round, just
above us. We could see how
beautiful she was, and how her
feathers gleamed in the sunshine,
but she didn't fly down to the
Pearl Palace lake.

King Everest strode forward, looking very anxious. "Princess Diamonde," he ordered, "please read your poem!"

Diamonde curtsied. As she unrolled her scroll I saw Gruella standing next to Fairy G, and to my absolute amazement they winked at each other!

"Once upon a time there were two very beautiful princesses—" Diamonde began.

And then she stopped. A shower of tiny stars was sparkling all round her head, and when I looked at Fairy G she was smiling hugely, and holding her wand up in the air.

"Oh NO!" Diamonde squealed, "what's happening?"

And I could see the words fading

from the paper she was holding...fading away until the paper was as blank as mine had been!

Fairy G stomped out from the crowd, Gruella following closely behind her.

"It's called 'Getting a Taste of Your Own Medicine', Princess Diamonde," she boomed loudly.

"Gruella told me exactly what you did to Sarah. Now, you have just one chance to save the day. Is there anything you'd like to say?"

Diamonde went quite white, and hung her head. "I'm very, very sorry," she muttered, and then she burst into tears and rushed away.

And as she ran, the Silver Swan flew gracefully down to the Pearl Palace lake.

As she landed, Hannah pushed me. "Go on!" she hissed.

"You too!" I whispered back. "ALL of us!"

So all of us in Lily Room
walked towards the Silver Swan.
We curtsied deeply, and I began,
"Silver Swan, we welcome you!"

"Flying down to water blue,"
Hannah went on, and we recited

the whole poem without a single mistake. As we finished the swan bowed her beautiful silver head, and King Everest gave a signal to the musicians...

And we began our dance of welcome. When we'd finished, our headteacher clapped his hands for silence.

"Thank you, thank you!" he said. "And now, ladies and

gentlemen, I have much pleasure in announcing the winners of the Silver Swan Award. There is no doubt in my mind that the princesses who have done the most for Pearl Palace are..."

He paused, and we waited for what seemed like AGES...

"Lily Room!"

Chapter Six

We could hardly believe our ears –
but when the cheering started we
laughed and we cried and we
hugged each other over and over
again. And then Fairy Angora and
Fairy G presented each of us with
the most gorgeous Pearl Sash, and
we led the procession back to Pearl
Palace...and the Celebration Ball!

The ball was utterly, utterly
GLORIOUS. Strings of pearls
were hung on every wall, and
there were bunches of pearly roses
on every table. Stars twinkled

from the ceiling, and we danced every single dance until we were out of breath and our feet were aching. It was FABULOUS...the most wonderful evening ever.

"What a brilliant way to end the term," Lucy said happily as we finally made our way up the stairs to bed, and she was SO right...

And although it was sad to think we weren't going to see each other over the holidays, we had something VERY special to look forward to.

EMERALD CASTLE!

And please please pretty please – make sure you're there too!

What happens next in

Emerald Castle?

Meet the Daffodil Room princesses in:

Princess Amelia
and the Silver Seal

Princess Leah
and the Golden Seahorse

Princess Ruby
and the Enchanted Whale

Princess Millie
and the Magical Mermaid

Princess Rachel
and the Dancing Dolphin

Princess Zoe
and the Wishing Shell

This Christmas, look out for

PRINCESS PARADE
ISBN 978 1 84616 504 7

Two stories in one book

Win a Tiara Club
Perfect Princess Prize!

Look for the secret word in mirror writing that is hidden in a tiara in each of the Tiara Club books. Each book has one word. Put together the six words from books **19** to **24** to make a special Perfect Princess sentence, then send it to us together with 20 words or more on why you like the Tiara Club books. Each month, we will put the correct entries in a draw and one lucky reader will receive a magical Perfect Princess prize!

Send your Perfect Princess sentence,
at least 20 words on why you like the Tiara Club,
your name and your address on a postcard to:
THE TIARA CLUB COMPETITION,
Orchard Books, 338 Euston Road,
London, NW1 3BH

Australian readers should write to:
Hachette Children's Books,
Level 17/207 Kent Street, Sydney, NSW 2000.

Only one entry per child.
Final draw: 30 September 2008

By Vivian French
Illustrated by Sarah Gibb

The Tiara Club

PRINCESS CHARLOTTE
AND THE BIRTHDAY BALL   ISBN   978 1 84362 863 7

PRINCESS KATIE
AND THE SILVER PONY   ISBN   978 1 84362 860 6

PRINCESS DAISY
AND THE DAZZLING DRAGON   ISBN   978 1 84362 864 4

PRINCESS ALICE
AND THE MAGICAL MIRROR   ISBN   978 1 84362 861 3

PRINCESS SOPHIA
AND THE SPARKLING SURPRISE   ISBN   978 1 84362 862 0

PRINCESS EMILY
AND THE BEAUTIFUL FAIRY   ISBN   978 1 84362 859 0

The Tiara Club at Silver Towers

PRINCESS CHARLOTTE
AND THE ENCHANTED ROSE   ISBN   978 1 84616 195 7

PRINCESS KATIE
AND THE DANCING BROOM   ISBN   978 1 84616 196 4

PRINCESS DAISY
AND THE MAGICAL MERRY-GO-ROUND   ISBN   978 1 84616 197 1

PRINCESS ALICE
AND THE CRYSTAL SLIPPER   ISBN   978 1 84616 198 8

PRINCESS SOPHIA
AND THE PRINCE'S PARTY   ISBN   978 1 84616 199 5

PRINCESS EMILY
AND THE WISHING STAR   ISBN   978 1 84616 200 8

The Tiara Club at Ruby Mansions

PRINCESS CHLOE
AND THE PRIMROSE PETTICOATS   ISBN   978 1 84616 290 9

PRINCESS JESSICA
AND THE BEST-FRIEND BRACELET   ISBN   978 1 84616 291 6

PRINCESS GEORGIA
AND THE SHIMMERING PEARL   ISBN   978 1 84616 292 3

PRINCESS OLIVIA
AND THE VELVET CLOAK   ISBN   978 1 84616 293 0

PRINCESS LAUREN
AND THE DIAMOND NECKLACE   ISBN   978 1 84616 294 7

PRINCESS AMY
AND THE GOLDEN COACH   ISBN   978 1 84616 295 4

The Tiara Club at Pearl Palace

PRINCESS HANNAH AND THE LITTLE BLACK KITTEN	ISBN	978 1 84616 498 9
PRINCESS ISABELLA AND THE SNOW-WHITE UNICORN	ISBN	978 1 84616 499 6
PRINCESS LUCY AND THE PRECIOUS PUPPY	ISBN	978 1 84616 500 9
PRINCESS GRACE AND THE GOLDEN NIGHTINGALE	ISBN	978 1 84616 501 6
PRINCESS ELLIE AND THE ENCHANTED FAWN	ISBN	978 1 84616 502 3
PRINCESS SARAH AND THE SILVER SWAN	ISBN	978 1 84616 503 0
BUTTERFLY BALL	ISBN	978 1 84616 470 5
CHRISTMAS WONDERLAND	ISBN	978 1 84616 296 1
PRINCESS PARADE	ISBN	978 1 84616 504 7

All priced at £3.99.
Butterfly Ball, Christmas Wonderland and *Princess Parade* are priced at £5.99.
The Tiara Club books are available from all good bookshops, or can be ordered
direct from the publisher: Orchard Books, PO BOX 29, Douglas IM99 IBQ.
Credit card orders please telephone 01624 836000
or fax 01624 837033 or visit our website: www.orchardbooks.co.uk
or e-mail: bookshop@enterprise.net for details.

To order please quote title, author and ISBN and your full name and address.
Cheques and postal orders should be made payable to 'Bookpost plc.'
Postage and packing is FREE within the UK
(overseas customers should add £2.00 per book).

Prices and availability are subject to change.

Check out

website at:

www.tiaraclub.co.uk

You'll find Perfect Princess games and fun things to do, as well as news on the Tiara Club and all your favourite princesses!